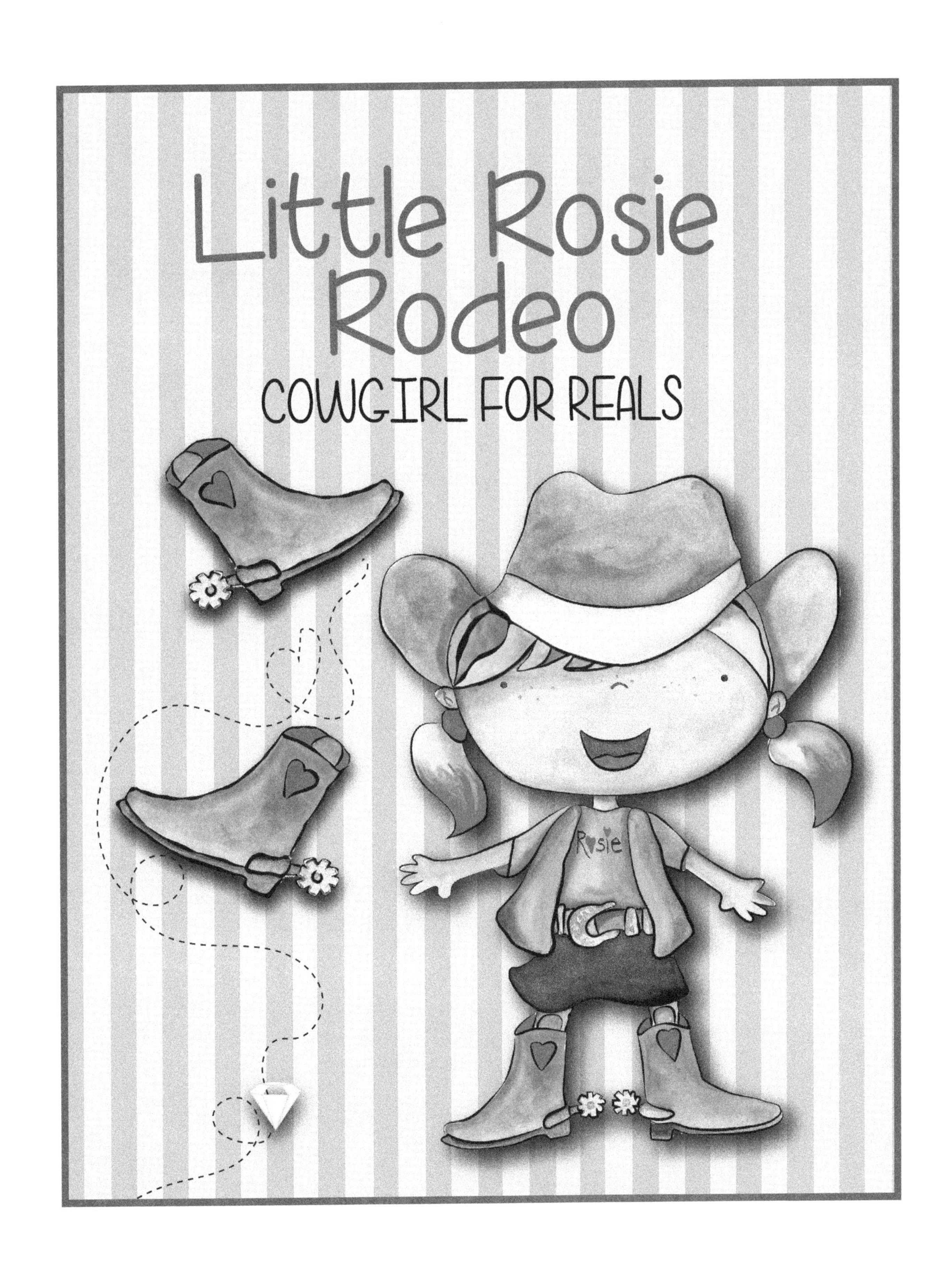

Lexi Kinney

Little Rosie Rodeo

Written by Lexi Kinney
Illustrated by Marinella Aguirre
ISBN 978-1-948543-55-2

Printed in the United States of America

To Ella Rae, our little cowgirl, who will grow up knowing that cowboy boots work for any occasion!

I'm Little Rosie Rodeo,
a cowgirl for reals.
Pink hat on my head,
sparkly spurs on my heels.

I dream as I stare
out my window at night
of rodeo buckles
that twinkle with light.

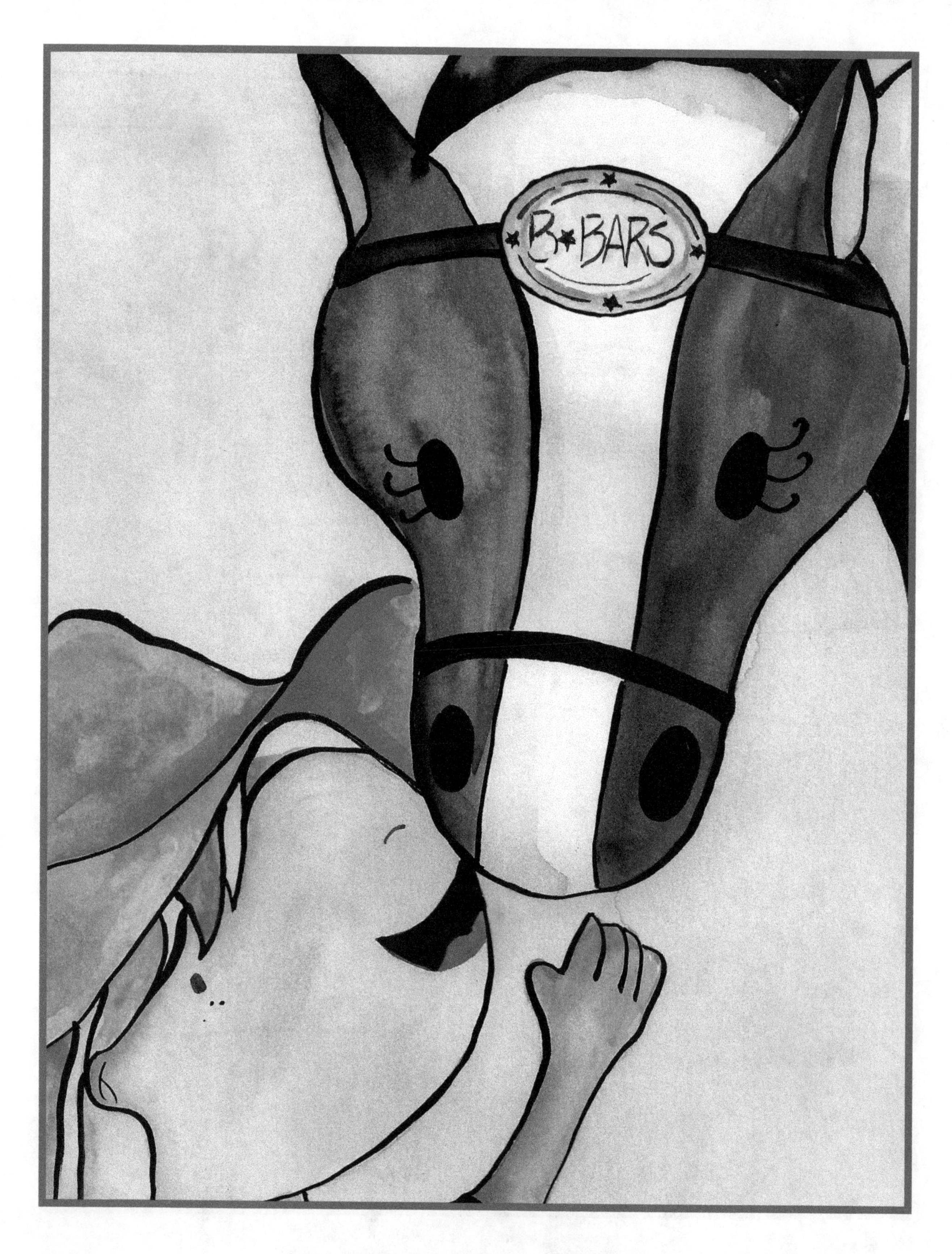

My best friend's B-Bars,
it can't be denied!
We're rodeo partners
who work side by side.

What can we do,
me and B-Bars?
We want to win buckles
that sparkle like stars!

Barrel racing is first,
the start of the day.
B-Bars is so happy
he lets out a NEIGH!

My buddy B-Bars
is ready to go.
He'll zig and he'll zag
until I say WHOA!

Two pigtails that glow
like red burning flames.
We race through the dirt
in these rodeo games.

What else can we do,
me and B-Bars?
We want to win buckles
that sparkle like stars!

A goat tying race
for my best friend and me.
When this run is over,
they'll set that goat free.

B-Bars throws his brakes
and my feet hit the ground.
Dismounting in motion,
our favorite playground.

A quick little flip
gets that goat on the ground.
I grab three of his feet
and wrap that string 'round.

I take three steps back,
my hands in the air!
A real cowgirl smiles
with dirt in her hair!

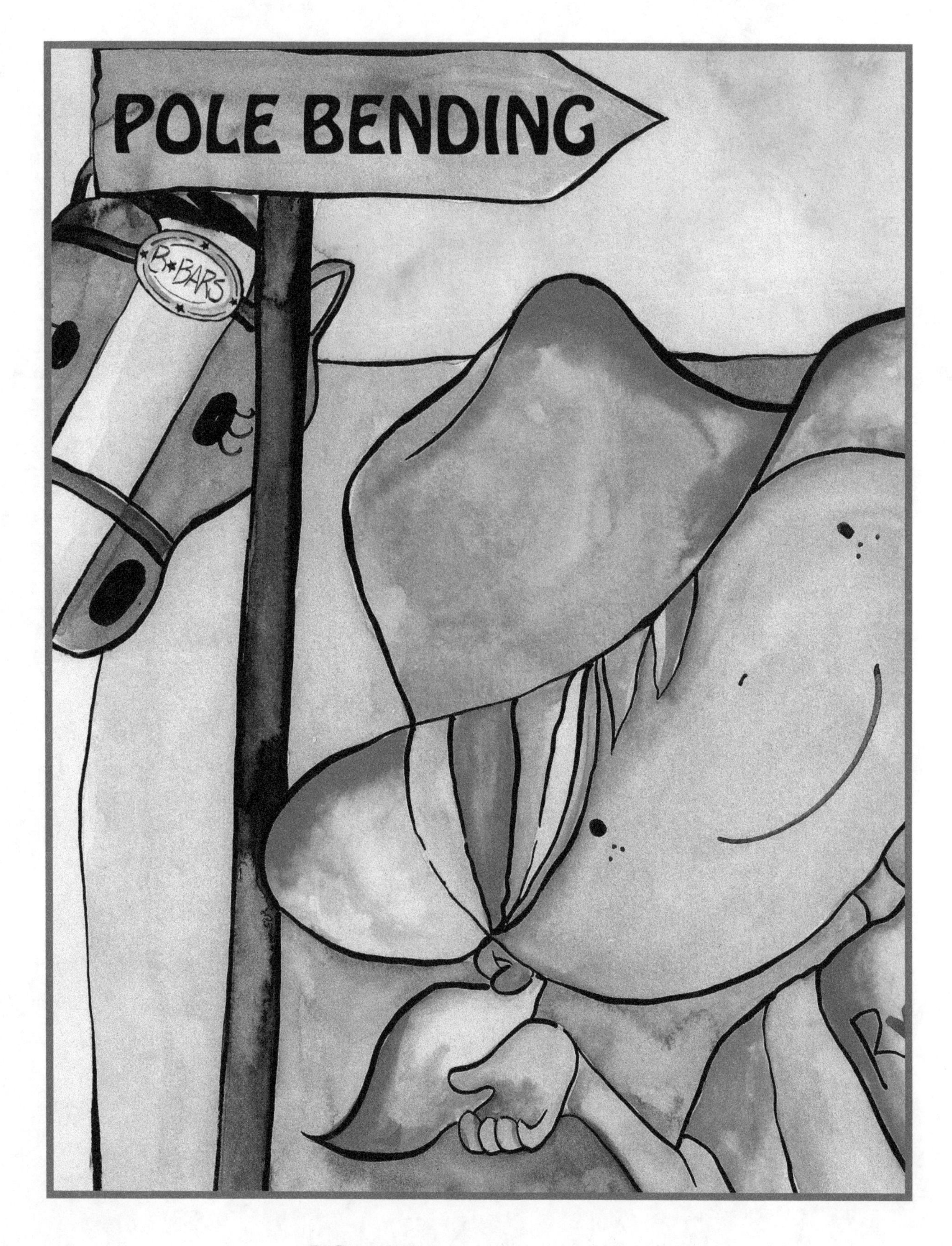

What else can we do,
me and B-Bars?
We want to win buckles
that sparkle like stars!

Zig zaggin' around,
the next race of the day.
Pole bending's so fun.
B-Bars neighs, HOORAY!

With a good running start,
his nose crosses the line.
The big clock begins
to track our best time.

We swing 'round those poles
lined up in a row.
Like a square dance we ride
in a fun do-si-do.

We zig to the left,
and we zig to the right.
We leave every pole standing.
I'm hangin' on tight!

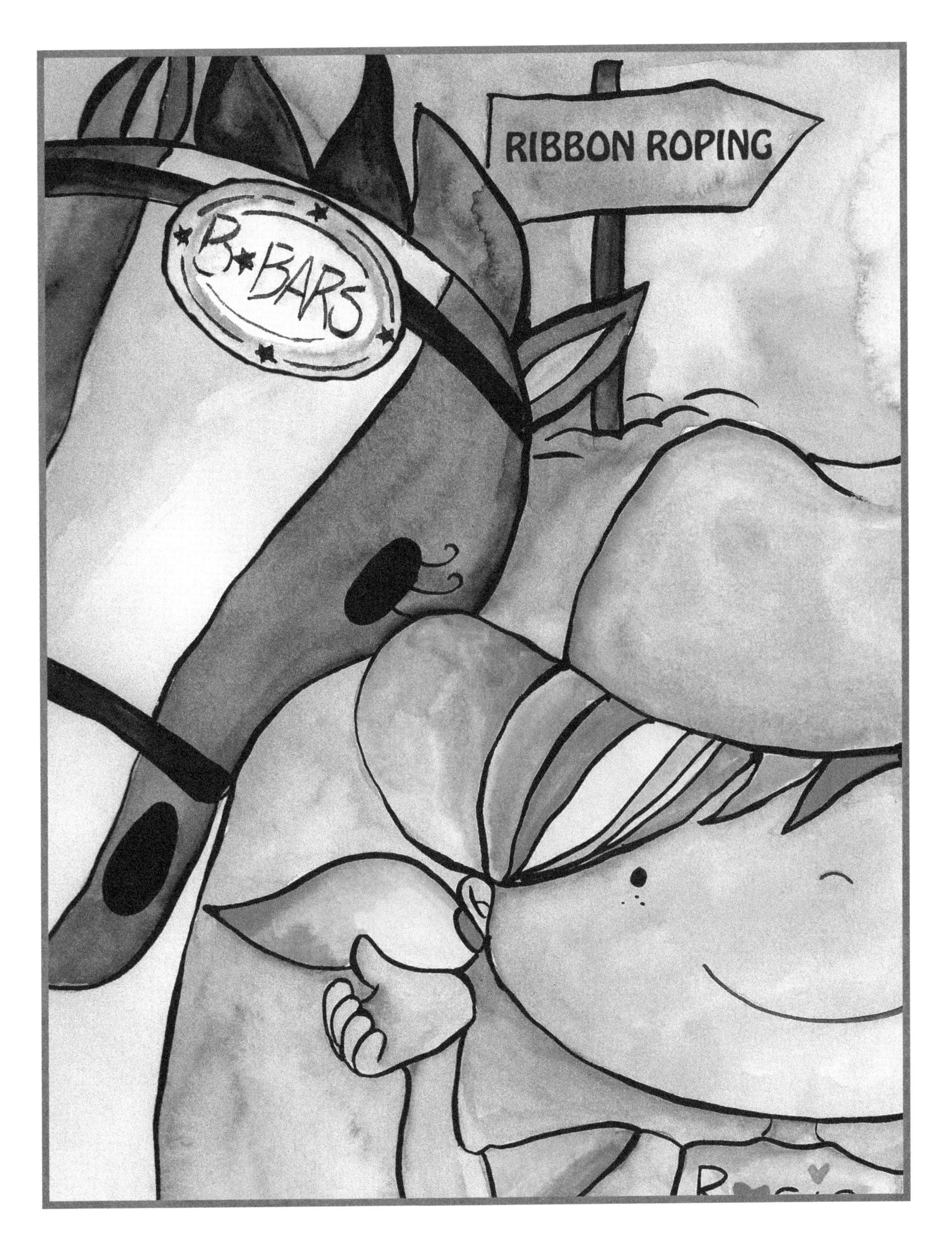

What else can we do,
me and B-Bars?
We want to win buckles
that sparkle like stars!

Ribbon roping is next,
last race of the day.
B-Bars thinks that it's silly,
but still neighs, OKAY!

A red ribbon tied
to a calf that is stray.
Every time I get close,
that calf runs away!

The roper comes by
and helps in this race.
Otherwise, I'd be running
all over the place!

Together we pull
from the tail of that calf,
the red ribbon tied.
Then we giggle and laugh.

Eyes on the finish,
I'm earning my place.
Kicking dirt in the air
with a smile on my face.

So proud of us two,
me and B-Bars.
We won us some buckles
that sparkle like stars!

The rodeo's over.
We parade off the dirt.
My buckle's still shining,
though there's dust on my shirt!

I'll remember this day
with me and B-Bars.
So many buckles
that sparkle like stars!

Beautiful buckles,
I want to win more.
But even better than buckles...
it's B-Bars I adore!

Most comfortable in jeans and cowboy boots, Lexi Kinney is an LA city girl with a cowgirl's heart. Lexi has ten siblings, and is mother to five and granny to five. As the author of four picture books—*Little Rosie Rodeo, Buckaroo Chuck, Animal Jax* and *Little Joe Smileyhead*—she draws from her many life experiences to inspire children everywhere.

Born in Venezuela, Marianella Aguirre has been a world traveler since she was a young girl. She loved making sketches during travels with her mother and to this day many countries' cultures are reflected in her drawings. She has illustrated over twenty published books in both English and Spanish. Marianella and her husband currently reside in New Zealand.

CPSIA information can be obtained
at www.ICGtesting.com
Printed in the USA
LVHW061431180420
653961LV00011B/1104